Snow Baby

Written by
Jane Street

Illustrated by
Charlene Yandell

Copyright © 2002 By Jane Street
Illustrations by Charlene Yandell

Available from:

Parkway Publishers, Inc.
P. O. Box 3678
Boone, NC 28607
Phone/Fax: (828) 265-3993
www.parkwaypublishers.com

Library of Congress Cataloging-in-Publication Data

Street, Jane.
    Snow Baby / by Jane Street; Illustrated by Charlene Yandell.
    p. cm.
    Summary: Based on the true story of a horse, that, despite being bred a race-horse, shows her true beauty in loyal and loving service to children.
    ISBN 1-887905-56-1
    [1. Horses--Fiction. 2. Animals--Infancy--Fiction. 3. Tennessee--Fiction.] I. Yandell, Charlene, ill. II. Title.
    PZ7.S9152 Sn 2002
    [Fic]--dc21

                                                              2002002944

Editing: Julie Shissler and Carolyn Howser
Layout and Cover Design: Aaron Burleson

Snow Baby

FOR LAURIE

Snow Baby

CHAPTER ONE

It was Christmas Eve, and the first snow of the season was beginning to fall on the hills of eastern Tennessee. The lights from the barn at Abberton Farm reflected off the snow-covered ground as people hurriedly came from different areas of the farm to see and welcome the newborn white filly.

"Look at her legs!" said her proud owner.

"Bet she'll be very fast!" said the head trainer.

"We'll see," said the vet.

The owner named the new filly Abberton's Christmas Snow, but she was soon given the nickname Snow Baby by the farmhands and trainers.

Snow Baby did not actually see the snowfall for which she was named. She was born in a warm barn with roomy stalls and soft, sweet smelling straw for a bed.

From the day Snow Baby was born, she had a special friend at Abberton Farm. His name was Jeff. He had grown up on the farm and became a horse trainer. Jeff was assigned as Snow Baby's trainer and began to spend time with her every day. He knew gentle ways to win her trust. He spoke softly to her and rubbed her neck and withers. She soon knew his voice, and he always spoke to her before entering her stall so she was never startled.

One day while she was still young, Jeff brought a small halter with him into Snow Baby's stall. He was careful to talk to her and let her see and smell the halter before slipping it over her nose, over her ears, and buckling it under her chin. Snow Baby did not mind. She had seen her mother wear a halter so she was not afraid.

Snow Baby was gentle and good, and everyone at Abberton Farm loved her. Her life was happy.

But all babies grow up, including baby horses. One day Jeff came to move her away from her mother, away from her comfortable, roomy stall with the soft hay floor, and into a new and strange place.

Snow Baby's new home was the training barn. It was the biggest building Snow Baby had ever seen. In the center was a large area where Jeff exercised and trained the horses when the weather was bad. Each horse had a large stall surrounding the exercise area so that it could watch the others train. Snow Baby watched but didn't really understand much of what she saw.

Often Jeff came and talked to her as the other horses trained. She didn't really know what he was saying most of the time, but she loved Jeff's visits.

The best time of all was when the weather turned sunny and warm. Snow Baby was turned out into the paddock to frolic with all the other yearlings at Abberton Farm. The first time she saw the pasture in spring she thought she would burst with excitement! She had been outside many times, but had never seen the pasture without a blanket of snow.

If Snow Baby had been able to see and recognize color, she would have seen deep green grass covering the hills. But horses do not see color. Instead, Snow Baby was aware of the warm breeze, the softness of the grass beneath her hooves, the butterflies flitting from flower to flower along the fence. And, Oh! the smell! Sweet, like new hay, but also fresh and clean, like the air just after a big rain.

One day Jeff brought a strange new object to Snow Baby's stall. As always, he was careful to begin talking to Snow Baby before he came into her stall so she would not be startled. He let Snow Baby sniff the new object which he called a blanket. Then he put it on Snow Baby's back. She did not mind. She had watched the older horses train and knew that they sometimes had something on their backs. She felt grown up and important because she was now old enough to go into the training area and begin her schooling.

She was first given a big breakfast of oats. Then Jeff attached a long rope to her halter and led her to the training ring. Snow Baby was so excited she could hardly keep from kicking and prancing. She wanted everyone to see that she was now in the training ring, and most of the people at the farm did see. The owner and his wife had come to watch Snow Baby's first day of training. As Jeff stood in the center of the ring, leading Snow Baby on the long rope, more and more of the trainers and workers gathered to watch.

Snow Baby went around the ring at a brisk trot, trying hard to understand Jeff's instructions and to follow them perfectly.

"Look at her go!" said the owner.

"Isn't she pretty?" said the owner's wife.

"She certainly is a special little filly," said the workers.

After her workout, Jeff took her out-

side, removed her blanket, and gave her a nice warm bath with a soapy sponge and a pail of water. He then walked her around while her coat dried. She was covered with a light blanket and put back into her stall.

The owner and his wife came by to say "Well done, Snow Baby." and to rub her neck. Snow Baby was so proud. She was given a snack of oats and left to rest. "Think, Snow Baby," Jeff said to her. "Remember our workout. Remember what you have learned."

Late afternoon was playtime in the paddock. The yearlings were free to romp and play. Sometimes they would race to the fence. Sometimes they would see who could kick the highest. Sometimes they would all stand together and watch the sunset. Then they were led back into the barn, groomed and fed. Blankets were put on all the horses and lights turned out.

Snow Baby was tired after her exciting day, and welcomed her warm cozy stall.

CHAPTER TWO

By early fall two things had happened that changed Snow Baby's life. First, her beautiful white color had become a dull gray. Oh, she was still called Snow Baby, but her coat no longer looked like fresh fallen snow; more like older snow piled by the side of the road where dirt and fumes from cars had settled. The second thing was more serious. The trainers at Abberton Farm began to suspect that she would not become a racehorse.

"At this point in her training she should be faster," said the owner.

"She seems distracted," said the chief trainer.

"It's just that she is so curious about everything," said Jeff.

"Her legs don't seem to be growing quite as long as I expected," said the veterinarian.

It was true that Snow Baby's legs weren't quite as long and as slender as the other yearlings. She was slow when running at play. She seemed to deliberately let the others go first, as though she would rather follow. This was serious because Abberton Farm raised racehorses.

Year-end trials were coming up. This was the time for all the young horses to compete against each other to decide who would continue race-training and who would be sold.

Race day came. All the trainers came to watch. Neighbors from surrounding farms came to inspect the new racehorses. Snow Baby saw all her playmates from the paddock. The big red horse named King Neptune was led into the first gate. Next was Moonglow, a dappled gray filly who was Snow Baby's training partner. Next, Snow Baby was led into the starting gate. It was narrow and high, so that she could see nothing but the track in front of her. She had been in the starting gate many times and knew to stand still as the other horses were loaded in on either side of her.

Some of the horses were nervous and excited. A little brown colt named Shakespeare was led in circles to calm him down so he could be placed into the gate next to Snow Baby. The last horse to be loaded was a sleek black colt name Blazing Star.

Snow Baby stood quietly waiting for the doors to open and the bell to sound. All her playmates were there with her. She was excited about the new game. When all the horses were in place there was a hush as horses, riders, and spectators all waited for the starting bell to ring. Suddenly the bell rang, the gates opened, and the race began.

Snow Baby sprang from the gate and ran as hard as she could. King Neptune was running right beside her. Blazing Star was four horses back behind Shakespeare and Moonglow. By the time the horses had reached the halfway point King Neptune had fallen behind. He was a big horse and not nearly as fast as the smaller ones. Blazing Star had moved past Moonglow, and Snow Baby and Shakespeare were running neck and neck. By the three quarter pole Snow Baby felt herself slowing down. She tried to make herself keep running, but no matter how badly she wanted it, her legs just could not keep going.

Blazing Star turned on a burst of speed and ran by her. Shakespeare and Moonglow passed her. Even King Neptune caught and passed her. When the race was over, Blazing Star had won, Moonglow had finished a close second with Shakespeare right behind, and Snow Baby had finished last.

The time had come to decide which horses would continue training, and which would leave Abberton Farm. King Neptune was sold to a farmer who lived over in North Carolina. Moonglow and Shakespeare were to be given a chance. As for Blazing Star, it was obvious that he was well named indeed. He was certainly blazing fast, faster than any horse Abberton Farm had ever trained. It seemed that he was destined to be a star.

All the workers at the farm were excited about Blazing Star and his promise of greatness, but they were also afraid that the owner would decide to sell Snow Baby any day.

No one wanted her to leave Abberton Farm. Every person loved her, but they all knew that she just did not fit in. What to do with Snow Baby became a major topic of conversation among the people of Abberton Farm.

"Maybe she could be a lead pony, and lead the racehorses to the starting gate," said Jeff.

"No, she doesn't like to lead. She seems more comfortable following," said the chief trainer.

"I know," said the owner's wife, "We could teach her to pull a wagon. All our grandchildren and their friends would enjoy riding around the farm in a wagon when they come to visit. Snow Baby is so gentle and she loves people."

"She would be perfect!" said the owner.

So instead of becoming the snow-white racehorse that everyone had expected her to be, Snow Baby would become a wagon horse. But she was gentle and good, and wanted to do please the people of Abberton Farm, so she began learning to pull a wagon.

Life changed abruptly for Snow Baby.

She no longer lived in the big, roomy stall with a view of the training area. Her home was now a much smaller stall off to the side of the big training arena. This was where the lead ponies were kept, the non-racing horses whose job it is to lead the racehorses to the starting gates. The best part of Snow Baby's day was Jeff's morning visit, before he went to the training ring. He always had a special snack for her. Snow Baby would no longer be a part of the training routine in the big arena. She couldn't even watch the other horses train. After all, what did a wagon horse need with a view of the training area?

She was fed each morning and led outside, no longer to the race-training ring but to the big, bare area in front of the hay barn. She was strapped into a harness instead of the lightweight racing saddle she had become used to.

The harness was big and awkward. A large collar was hung around her neck. Snow Baby could feel a small strap going the entire length of her back from her neck to her tail. Hanging from this was a strap draped over her hips and another around her rump. These straps, along with the belt around her belly, were where the side rails of the wagon would be attached.

In addition to all these, there was another small strap called a breastplate which went from the collar down between her front legs and was then attached to the girth. All these straps rubbed and tickled. They did not hurt Snow Baby, but they did startle her sometimes.

She was led around dragging a small log. This was to teach her to turn slowly. Many times she heard "Snow Baby, slow down." "You will turn the wagon over if you turn that fast." The reason she made a quick turn was to see behind her. After all, she was used to having commands whispered in her ear, not yelled from somewhere behind the old log that she was dragging.

The worst thing of all was that Jeff was no longer her trainer. Snow Baby's training was turned over to Old Harry, the farm manager.

Old Harry was kind, but Snow Baby did not understand all the sudden changes in her life. Still, she was a good horse and worked hard to learn and to do her job well. No one came to watch Snow Baby learn to pull the little red wagon which had been bought for the grandchildren, but she practiced every day, until she knew the way to control the wagon's movement.

Time passed slowly for Snow Baby. She was alone much of the time and playing in the fields wasn't as much fun as it had been when she was playing with Blazing Star and the other yearlings.

Finally the day came for Snow Baby to show how well she had learned her lessons. It was Thanksgiving. The owner's grandchildren had come to visit. Old Harry led Snow Baby out to the barnyard and hitched the harness to the little red wagon. Happy and cheering children eagerly climbed in, and with Old Harry driving, took their first ride with Snow Baby.

The trails through the woods were covered with soft fall leaves that rustled and crunched as Snow Baby walked. The children yelled. "Go, Snow Baby!" but she never went too fast. She had learned to obey Old Harry's commands, and knew that she must never pull the wagon faster than a gentle trot.

During the Thanksgiving weekend each day began for the children with breakfast, and a ride around the farm in the wagon. "We love you, Snow Baby," they would say. "You are our special horse."

How sad it was to say goodbye when the children left! "We have to go home now, Snow Baby," they said. "We have to go back to school, but we will see you at Christmas."

The days between Thanksgiving and Christmas stretched very long. Jeff came by every day to rub her neck and talk to her. She welcomed the days when Old Harry hitched her to the wagon to practice, and she looked forward to the children's return.

CHAPTER THREE

As winter came and snow began to fall, training for the racehorses was moved indoors to the big arena at the center of the barn. The townspeople came more and more to watch Blazing Star train. There was much excited talk about what would happen next spring when he was old enough to enter races.

"Blazing Star will win every race!" said a gray headed lady who was watching the training.

"Our town will be famous!" said an elderly gentleman.

"We will have to put up a sign," said the mayor. "Home of the world famous champion, Blazing Star."

"We will see," said the owner, but his big smile told everyone that he too thought that Blazing Star would be a champion and he was very proud.

One day the mayor of the town said, "We need something new and exciting for our town Christmas party. We need a big party in the town square for the children."

"Why don't you invite the children to decorate the town tree?" asked the owner. "Snow Baby could pull the tree into town on the little red wagon."

What a wonderful idea!" said the owner's wife. "We can decorate the wagon with bells and greenery."

The mayor agreed, and so it was that a town tradition began. When the appointed day arrived, the little red wagon was decked out with branches of sweet smelling cedar, bright red holly berries, and brass sleigh bells. Snow Baby's harness was also decorated with red bows and bells. The town council selected a huge pine tree which the workers at Abberton Farm cut and loaded into the wagon. Old Harry climbed into the driver's seat, and with a click of his tongue and a gentle tap of the reins on Snow Baby's back, they set off for town.

What excitement there was in the town square! The children tried to be quiet and listen carefully for the jingle, jingle of Snow Baby's bells as she pulled the big evergreen tree closer and closer to town. Some of the children ran to the corner so they could watch the road which led from town to Abberton Farm.

"I think I can hear bells," said one little girl.

"Look! Here she comes!" yelled a little boy.

As Snow Baby rounded the corner to the town square a great cheer went up from the crowd. The men of the town unloaded the tree and placed it upright in a stand in the middle of the square. Snow

Baby watched as the children decked the tree with bells, stars. lights, and garlands. She felt very special to be a part of this joyful day.

After the decorating was done the children came by one after another to say, "What a good horse you are, Snow Baby," and "Thank you, Snow Baby." Many gave Snow Baby treats: a carrot, a sugar lump, or an apple.

All the children came by except one little girl. She was standing on the sidelines. She had not helped with decorating and had not joined the group of happy and excited children. She had two long braids hanging from under her hat and she looked sad and frightened.

No one paid any attention to her, nor even seemed to know that she was there. Snow Baby moved slowly toward the girl, as if to say hello. But Old Harry climbed back into the driver's seat and clucked to Snow Baby. It was time to take the empty wagon home.

Snow Baby looked back as they turned the corner. She wanted to remember the wonderful day and the important part she had played. There, standing in the shadows apart from the other children was the little girl with the long braids, watching as Snow Baby slowly walked away.

CHAPTER FOUR

Spring came, and with it the time for the first race of the season. All of Abberton Farm was buzzing with excitement. Brand new silks had been ordered for Blazing Star, Shakespeare, and Moonglow's debut.

Shakespeare's rider was wearing bright red with accents in yellow. Pale blue had been chosen for Moonglow, and Blazing Star's colors were purple and gold. "The colors of royalty," the owner said. His rider had a new purple silk shirt with a big, bright stripe of gold over one shoulder. Blazing Star was given a new purple blanket, soft as velvet, with his name embroidered on the side in gold.

On the morning of the race everyone on Abberton Farm was up before daylight, hurrying around, getting ready for the big day. As Blazing Star left the barn, he walked past Snow Baby's stall. It had become his habit to whinny softly to Snow Baby. They had been friends since their early training days, and continued to have respect for each other. Blazing Star seemed to be wishing Snow Baby could go with him.

The excitement of preparing for the big race sent everyone scurrying The horses must be carefully led into their trailers. The veterinarian had to be sure that he had all the neces-

sary supplies in case any of the horses should need medical attention. The new racing silks must be ironed and packed.

But the hustle and bustle getting ready for the race was nothing compared to the excitement when Blazing Star returned home with the first place trophy!

The owner called from the race track with the news that Blazing Star won. By the time the truck pulling Blazing Star's trailer came in through the main gate, a big crowd had assembled to welcome him home and celebrate the victory. Townspeople and all the trainers lined the fence along the drive to wave and cheer. Someone had made a big banner congratulating Blazing Star, and had hung it over the stable door.

Snow Baby watched the excitement from the paddock. It was time for her to go inside to be brushed and fed, but with all the excitement about Blazing Star, no one remembered. Blazing Star was led from the trailer as people clapped and cheered. The owner lifted the trophy high in the air for the crowd to see and admire.

Snow Baby looked around the crowd of people. and there, on the edge of the crowd, was the little girl with the long braids. She was not watching Blazing Star. She was not admiring the trophy. She was looking at Snow Baby. Snow Baby moved over to the fence. The little girl left the crowd and walked slowly towards the paddock.

"Privet Snezhok," she said in a timid voice that was not much more than a whisper. Snow Baby didn't understand the words, of course, not because they were spoken in a strange language. Snow Baby didn't understand words in English either except for her name, and a few commands.

What she did understand was the caring in the little girl's voice, and the gentle touch of her hand as she timidly rubbed Snow Baby's neck. She reached into her pocket, took something out, and held it towards Snow Baby.

Snow Baby saw what looked like a small rock with stripes on it. She sniffed it. It smelled sort of like sugar, but with a strange new smell that Snow Baby did not recognize. The children would have known it was peppermint candy, but Snow Baby had never seen candy before. She picked it up with her lips, being careful not to bite the little hand that offered it.

"Katia," called a voice from the crowd. "Katia, where are you? It's time to go." The little girl looked back in the direction of the crowd, then turned to Snow Baby. "Mne nado idti," she said. "Dovidania."

She gave Snow Baby a quick hug, turned and walked back towards the crowd. She turned one last time to look at Snow Baby and smiled a big smile. It seemed to Snow Baby that her whole face began to glow with happiness.

CHAPTER FIVE

As the years went by, Blazing Star lived up to all the hopes and dreams of his owner. He won every race that he entered. The trophy cabinet in the barn began to overflow. His picture was on the cover of *Racing Today* magazine. News of his racing triumphs appeared weekly in the town newspaper. There was even some talk of erecting a statue of him in the town square.

Snow Baby did not win races but she loved the summertime when all the children came to visit. Every day she was hitched to the wagon and happy and excited children would climb in and take a tour. After the ride, the children would give her a carrot or an apple. They would rub her neck and say, "You're a good horse, Snow Baby." Snow Baby felt special and important. But fall would come, school would begin again, and all the children would go home.

Snow Baby was put out to pasture, and not called on again until Christmas, when once again she was hitched to the wagon to bring the town Christmas tree to the square. She would be dressed with bells and bows, and the wagon would be decorated with greenery, and the whole town would come to watch the big event. On that day, Snow Baby felt very beautiful and very special. After Christmas, she was once again put out to pasture. It was hard to wait for summer and the coming of the children.

Only Katia came to see her. She came almost every day and sat on the fence of the paddock rubbing Snow Baby's neck. At first she did not speak often, and when she did, she spoke in Russian. She always brought a small piece of peppermint for Snow Baby. Snow Baby would smell the peppermint the minute Katia came into the barn. Only Katia brought her peppermint; only Katia knew she loved it.

Snow Baby loved to see Katia smile. She didn't smile much at first. She was a small child. She had spent most of her life in an orphanage in a small country north of Russia called Laplandia. She was adopted and brought to America by a couple who had no children.

She was so grateful to have a lovely home and a room of her own, because, in the orphanage, she was sleeping in a room with eleven other girls. She really loved her new family, but everything in America was strange.

For one thing, no one in the entire town knew how to speak Russian, the only language that Katia knew. The children at school tried to be nice but she couldn't understand what they said. The teacher moved Katia to the front of the class, and tried to help her learn English, but when she attempted to speak English, no one understood her words. After a while the other children stopped trying to be friendly.

They did not intend to be rude, but they did not know how to make her understand. How can you play freeze tag with someone who doesn't know the rules and cannot understand when you try to teach them? How can you play Barbie with someone who doesn't know who Barbie is?

Katia was left alone more and more. How she missed having a friend that she could sit and talk to! Maybe she might be invited to parties and go to movies if she only knew the new language. Instead, she found a wonderful and gentle friend in Snow Baby, where language was not needed.

Katia would sit on the pasture fence and talk softly to Snow Baby. She would sing songs she remembered from Laplandia. It did not matter that Snow Baby could not understand the words. Snow Baby understood the love in Katia's voice, and Katia always had a piece of peppermint for Snow Baby.

Her mother and father worried that she spent too much time with Snow Baby, but Katia would come home each day from Abberton Farm with a big smile on her face. When Katia smiled, her whole face lit up.

Jeff noticed the little blond girl who seemed to be there every day. One day he was waiting for Katia with a saddle and bridle on Snow Baby.

"Would you like to ride?" Jeff asked.

Katia was not sure she understood what he said, but he seemed to be motioning for her to get up into the saddle, so she timidly nodded and climbed on. Jeff led Snow Baby slowly around the riding ring while Katia held on to Snow Baby's mane.

Slowly, Katia learned to ride. She learned to say "whoa" and "go." Jeff taught her to groom Snow Baby.

"You must never put your horse up without a good brushing," he said.

Katia loved to brush Snow Baby, and even after she learned to speak English very well, she still sang to Snow Baby in her native language. She knew that Snow Baby didn't care what language she used. Snow Baby only cared that Katia hugged her neck and sang to her, and that Katia smiled more and more.

Over the next few years Katia and Snow Baby became almost inseparable. Jeff taught Katia how to ride Snow Baby bareback – not fast for racing, but a gentle trot across a field. They would take a slow walk up a creek, or a short but brisk run through a meadow, not for trophies or prizes but just for the love of riding and of being together.

CHAPTER SIX

When Katia started high school, she began playing soccer on the school team. She joined the swim team. She began marching with the flag corps. With so many after school rehearsals, she had less time to spend with Snow Baby.

She managed to visit every week and when she did, the two of them would gallop across the pasture, stop on the highest ridge and watch clouds go by. Katia would sing to Snow Baby, and always brought her a piece of peppermint.

Then one day Katia went away to college, and the visits stopped.

Everyday life was so different now. Even the Christmas parade began to change. Snow Baby still pulled the wagon into town with the town tree, but not many people came to see the festivities. There was now a big shiny new mall just down the road, and there were many lights and exciting things in the store windows.

Many years went by, but Snow Baby never forgot Katia.

One day the owner and his wife decided that the time had come to sell Abberton Farm. The city was growing fast, and developers wanted to buy the farm to subdivide and build houses. There was to be a big auction to sell all the horses of Abberton Farm. Naturally, there was much interest in Blazing Star. He didn't race anymore, but he was famous all over the world, and many people came to bid for him. When he was led into the arena, a sigh of admiration was heard from the crowd, for he was as beautiful as ever. The bidding was active, and when it was over, Blazing Star had brought a large sum of money. He was led from the arena to the sound of loud cheers and thunderous applause.

Shakespeare also sold for a nice price. He had enjoyed a good racing career, although he never became the champion that Blazing Star had become. Moonglow had retired from racing years before, and now lived on a farm nearby.

One by one the horses were sold, all except Snow Baby. For the first time in her life, real fear gripped her heart. What was to become of her?

Was she too old to have any value at all? Was there no one who wanted her? Her joints were stiff and she got tired faster than when she was young, but she could still pull a wagon. She was so accustomed to pulling that wagon that she could do it, even without a driver. There must be someone who needed a good wagon horse.

She watched the last horse being led away. She was now alone in the barn. Despair began to settle over her like a shadow as she began to wonder if perhaps no one wanted her. She did not notice a group of people coming into the barn. She was not aware of the crowd gathering outside her stall until she heard someone say, "Hi, Snow Baby! Remember me?"

She looked up and saw the owner, his wife, and a group of young adults, many of them with small children in their arms and on their shoulders. They crowded around her saying, "What a good horse you are!" Snow Baby did not recognize the grown-up faces, but she heard and remembered the loving voices. These were the children she had carried in her wagon all those wonderful summers. They were grown up now, but none had forgotten Snow Baby and the happy times at Abberton Farm.

Suddenly, she smelled something familiar, something which made her look around for a familiar face. There, on the edge of the crowd, smiling, was a little girl that looked like Katia. She was smaller than Snow Baby remembered Katia, and her hair was curls instead of braids, but she looked like Katia and even smelled of peppermint. This child could not be Katia. All the other children had grown up. Katia must have grown up too.

Snow Baby did not understand. Just then, the little girl's mother stepped forward. "Privet Snezhok," she said. "Snow Baby, you were my best friend when I had no friends. I can honestly say that I've never had a friend that has been as loyal to me, or that I've treasured more. This is my daughter, Anna. She wants to meet you, and she has something for you."

The little girl squealed with delight as Katia showed her how to hold the peppermint on her palm and offer it to Snow Baby.

One by one, the children of her past filed by her stall to introduce their children to Snow Baby. After all her friends had said hello, the mayor of the town stood to speak. He unrolled a scroll and began to read:

Whereas Snow Baby has proved
her strength and her courage by
always striving to do her best; and
whereas she has always set an
example for all of us by her hard
work and patience; and whereas she
has shown us the importance of love
in all that we do; and in recognition
of the fact that a beautiful life is one
that gives freely to others;

In appreciation, we, the town council
do hereby proclaim that this day
shall be celebrated each year as
'Snow Baby Day,' a day of caring,
in honor of Snow Baby and we
shall remember that true beauty lies
in the willingness to work to become
the best you can be at what you are
called to do. I furthermore
proclaim that Snow Baby is today
named our Official Village Horse.

Everyone clapped and cheered. Jeff brought a flower garland for her neck, with a beautiful pink and purple ribbon. Next the owner stood to make a speech.

"First, let me say how happy I am that you called me in time to stop the sale of Snow Baby in the auction. We have loved her so much through the years, and it warms our hearts to know that you have all loved her too. I appreciate your taking up money to buy her for your children, however, I cannot sell her to you. Instead, my wife and I would like to give Snow Baby to the children of the town. She will continue to give wagon rides in the summer and to bring the town tree at Christmas."

And so it is. If you go to the rolling hills of Tennessee today, to the place which was called Abberton Farm, you will still find Snow Baby giving the children rides in the wagon all summer. The children still bring apples and carrots and sometimes, peppermint. They say, "You're a good horse, Snow Baby," and "Snow Baby, I love you."

Every Christmas season begins with Snow Baby pulling the wagon with the town tree into the square for the children to decorate, and once every year, on Snow Baby Day, all the people of the town stop to remember and celebrate what true beauty really is.

Snow Baby